Once upon a time there were seven little boys.

They were always hungry.

One day their mother made a big pancake.

When the pancake was ready to eat, the seven hungry little boys said, 'Yum, yum, now we can eat you.'

'Uh oh,' thought the pancake. 'I do not want to be eaten by seven hungry little boys. I shall run away.'

So the pancake hopped out of the pan and rolled out of the door.

'Stop,' said the mother, and the seven hungry little boys said,

3

The big pancake rolled down the road.
After it ran the mother and the seven hungry
little boys.
'Stop,' said the mother, and the seven hungry
little boys said,

5

Soon the pancake met a horse.

'Stop,' said the horse. 'You look good to eat.'

'Oh no,' said the pancake. 'I do not want to be eaten by a horse,' and it rolled down the road.

'Stop,' said the horse.

'Stop,' said the mother, and the seven hungry little boys said,

Soon the pancake met a dog.

'Stop,' said the dog. 'You look good to eat.'

'Oh no,' said the pancake. 'I do not want to be eaten by a dog,' and it rolled down the road.

'Stop,' said the dog.

'Stop,' said the horse.

'Stop,' said the mother, and the seven hungry little boys said,

9

Soon the pancake met a cat.

'Stop,' said the cat. 'You look good to eat.'

'Oh no,' said the pancake. 'I do not want to be eaten by a cat,' and it rolled down the road.

'Stop,' said the cat.

'Stop,' said the dog.

'Stop,' said the horse.

'Stop,' said the mother, and the seven hungry little boys said,

But then the pancake met a fox.

'Stop,' said the fox.

'Oh no!' said the pancake.

'Oh no!' said the cat and the dog and the horse and the mother and the seven hungry little boys.

The fox tossed the pancake high up in the air.

He gobbled it up and he said,

Yum, yum